Toledo

Text, photographs, design, lay-out and printing
entirely created by the technical department of
EDITORIAL ESCUDO DE ORO, S.A.

Editorial Escudo de Oro, S.A.

Partial view of old Toledo, its houses clustering on the hillside over the River Tagus. At the top, the unmistakable silhouette of the Alcázar.

THE VISIT TO TOLEDO

To visit the labyrinth of narrow streets making up the old city of Toledo is to become immersed in what can rightly be called a museum-city, where at each step we encounter a monument and where each nook and cranny has its own history and legends. As the faithful reflection of its glorious past, this «City on the Tagus» has preserved practically intact an urban nucleus of an umistakable medieval fabric. This is the Toledo of the three cultures, a period marked by the cultural and religious co-existence of Moslems, Jews and Christians. The Mudéjar style is the artistic expression of this cultural co-existence and the one which best characterises the period. Nevertheless, Toledo had formerly been the capital of the Visigoth reign and the city of epoch-making councils, and was later to become inextricably associated

with El Greco. To quote Pérez Galdós, Toledo is a compendium of the history of Spain.
The guide you hold in your hands aims to be your travelling companion, and is structured into two large sections, devoted to the city and province respectively, as well as containing chapters on the history, festivities, the gastronomy, arts and crafts of Toledo. Each of the four itineraries forming the visit to the city is introduced by a plan showing the sights on it. Of these tourist routes, the first two are really indispensable, taking in as they do the city's most representative monuments. The third and fourth take the visitor to zones less well-known to tourists, though not for that less interesting.
The section devoted to Toledo province, which includes a complete road map, suggests three great routes. The first of these, the «Castle Route», takes us to various fortresses in the environs of Toledo, as well as such other outstanding monuments as the Hermitage of Santa María de Melque, one of the finest exponents of the Visigoth heritage. The second route leads us through the *comarca*, rural district, of La Sagra and on to the Mesa de Ocaña and the Toledan part of La Mancha. The third and final route is devoted particularly to Talavera de la Reina and Oropesa, lovely monumental sites in the west of the province.

Aerial view of Toledo.

Ruins of the Roman circus.

HISTORICAL INTRODUCTION

Situated in the centre of the Iberian Peninsula on a rocky promontory bordering the River Tagus, something which has always contributed to making this an impregnable stronghold, the origins of Toledo go back to the remotest times. Even before its occupation by the Romans in 192 BC, this was the important settlement of *Toletum*, forming part of Carpetania, an area populated by Celtic tribes. Already, Toledo was a key strategic point for the domination of the line marked out by the Tagus. The few remains unearthed from Roman times reveal the existence of a city of a considerable size, walled and with a sewage system certain sections of which remained in service until well into the 20th century. The ruins of the Roman circus in Vega Baja, accommodating over 30,000 spectators, further corroborates the status of Roman Toledo.
After crisis struck the Roman Empire, in 411 the city succumbed

with little serious resistance to the attack of the Alans, only to be conquered once more in 418 by the Visigoths who made it their capital, transferring the court here from Barcelona in the year 569. This marked the beginning of a period of political and religious splendour reflected in the celebration here of councils of resounding importance which played a crucial role both in the establishment of religious dogmas and of legal and political measures. Such is the case of the VIII Council of Toledo, held in 653, which produced the most important body of juridical rules of the period, the *Fuero Juzgo*. The I Council of Toledo, however, took place just before the Gothic conquest, in the year 400, whilst the III, in 589, celebrated the conversion of Recaredo from Arianism to Catholicism and, with it, the political and religious unification of Spain.
The arrival of the Moors on the Peninsula and in Toledo, in 711, marked the beginning of a period of enrichening cultural exchange thanks to the policy of religious tolerance. The peaceful co-existence of Moslems, Jews and Christians lasted after Toledo fell once more under Christian rule when it was reconquered by King Alphonse VI of Castile and León in the spring of 1085. This second phase of the «Toledo of the Three

The escutcheon of Toledo is found frequently throughout the city. Here, opposite the San Martín Gate.

The Mudéjar Church of Santiago del Arrabal.

Cultures», however, ended with the expulsion of the Jews decreed by the Catholic Monarchs in 1492 and, shortly afterwards, in 1502, of the Mudéjars.

It was particularly during this second period of co-existence between peoples and religions when the city enjoyed great cultural development. Thanks to this happy co-existence, though it was not completely free of conflict, Toledo began to stand out in many areas of science and art, becoming known as the intellectual centre of Europe. Perhaps the most important fruit of this melting-pot of cultures was the «Toledo School of Translators». Though no school existed as such, the term refers to the many scholars who, in the 12th and 13th centuries, translated Arabic works and the writings of such classical authors as Aristotle, Galen and Ptolemy, which had been lost to the western world and only existed in Arabic versions, building a veritable cultural bridge between Orient and Occident. This most important of labours, made possible thanks to the existence in Toledo of Jews and Mozarabs who knew both the Arabic and Latin languages, enjoyed the encouragement of such leading figures as King Alphonse X, the Wise. This was also the environment in which the Mudéjar style, which blends Christian and Moslem elements, was created. To this cultural splendour were added economic wealth and religious power. In 1088, shortly after the Christian conquest, Pope Urban II made Toledo the seat of the Spanish Catholic Church. The cathedral was installed in the main mosque, and it was not until 1226 that work on the present building began. The power of the Church was precisely what prevented an even greater decline when Philip II decided in 1561 to transfer the capital of the kingdom to Madrid. The imperial city continued to be the spiritual capital of Spain. The year 1983 marked the beginning of a great revival of the city's fortunes, however, with the creation of the Autonomous Community of Castile-La Mancha, of which Toledo is the capital. The importance of the medieval old city, preserved practically intact, and the important monumental heritage of Toledo in general, was given recognition in 1987, when UNESCO listed the city as part of World Heritage.

The old city of Toledo conserves its characteristic Moorish layout, with labyrinthine narrow streets.

OCAÑA
TALAVERA
ESCALONA
DIPUTACION
AVDA. DE LA RECONQUISTA
Ruinas del Circo Romano
AVDA. CARLOS III
CAMPO ESCOLAR
P. DEL CIRCO ROMANO
P. DE LOS CANONIGOS
GLORIETA DE LA RECONQUISTA
Puerta d o Antigua
AVDA. DE LA CABA
SANTIAGO
Pº. DE RECAREDO
CUESTA DE LA GRANJA
Palacio de la Diputación Provincial
Ermita del Cristo de la Vega
Nuncio Nuevo
Convento de Carmelitas Descalzas
CJON MERCED
BUZONES
Convento de las Capuchinas
REAL
PL. DE SANTA LEOCADIA
Santa Leocadia
LOS ALGIBES
DE LA MERCED
Torreón de los Abades
PL. STA. TERESA DE JESUS
Puerta del Cambrón
Santa Eulalia
Convento de Santo Domingo Antiguo
PUENTE DE LA CAVA
CTA. DE S. MARTIN
CAMBRON
Colegio de Doncellas
Casa de Mesa
SAN MARTIN
Cerro Virgen de la Gracia
Convento de San Clemente
S. CLEMENTE
San Román
Baño de la Cava
LA CAVA
San Juan de los Reyes
LAS BULAS
Mº de San Pedro Mártir
Casa de las Cadenas (Museo de Arte Contemporáneo)
REYES
Escuelas de Artes y Oficios
ANGEL
S. TOME
Santo Tomé
San Marc
STA. ANA
Sinagoga de Santa María la Blanca
Puente de San Martín
JUDERIA
CATOLICOS
PL. DEL CONDE
STA. URSUL
Taller del Moro
Museo Victorio Macho
Casa del Greco
Palacio de Fuensalida
Sinagoga del Tránsito
P. DE TRANSITO
ALAMILLOS
Río Tajo
EL CALVARIO
Convento de San Gil ó Gilitos
LOS DESCALZOS
CALVARIO
SAN CIPRIANO
San Cipriano
CARRERAS
Puerta de Adabaquín

LAS COVACHUELAS
LOS TRINITARIOS
HONDA
TAVERA
CARRETEROS
PL. HONDA
COVACHUELAS
ESPINO
PERALA
RIO LLANO
ESTACION DE AUTOBUSES
AVD. DE CASTILLA - LA MANCHA
Puente de Azarquiel
LA CARRERA
LA ANTEQUERUELA
PL. DE LA ANTEQUERUELA
PL. DE LOS ALFARES
AZACANES
GERARDO
LOBO
P. DE LA ROS
Puerta del Sol
Puerta de los Alarcones
CARRETAS
P. DEL MIRADERO
CUESTA DE ARMAS
Convento de San Pablo y Convento de la Purísima Concepción
Castillo de San Servando
Mezquita del Cristo de la Luz
CRISTO DE LA LUZ
ARCE
DOS CODOS
NUÑEZ
Convento de Santa Fe
Hospital y Museo de Santa Cruz
Puerta de Alcántara
Puente de Alcántara
LA SILLERIA
ALFILERITOS
CADENAS
Acueducto Romano
PL. DE LA CONCEPCION
Plaza de Zocodover
STA. FE
CERVANTES
LA PLATA
COMERCIO
P. DEL CARMEN
ALFERECES PROVISIONALES
PL. DE LA MAGDALENA
Mezquita de Tornerías
Corral de Don Diego
El Alcazar
HOMBRE DE PALO
J. LABRADOR
CUESTA DE CARLOS V
JUANELE
PUENTE NUEVO DE ALCANTARA
PLAZA MAYOR
Puerta de los Doce Cantos
La Catedral
Posada de la Hermandad
CARDENAL CISNEROS
PL. DEL SECO
San Miguel el Alto
PARRO
PL. DE S. JUSTO
LA CANDELARIA
VICARIO
BARCO
CTA. DE S. JUSTO
San Justo
Convento de San Juan de la Penitencia
CABESTREROS
PASEO DE LA CANDELARIA
AVE MARIA
POZO
SAN PABLO
Río Tajo
CIRCUNVALACION
CTA. DE
San Andrés
BAJADA DEL AMARGO
PLEGADERO
San Lucas
PASEO
Seminario
STA. CATALINA
BARCO
Casa del Diamantista
SEBASTIAN
Ermita Virgen del Valle
Parador Nacional

I. FROM NEW BISAGRA GATE TO THE CATHEDRAL

1. Tavera Hospital
2. Old Bisagra Gate
3. New Bisagra Gate, or Alphonse VI Gate
4. Church of Santiago del Arrabal
5. Mosque of Cristo de la Luz
6. Puerta del Sol
7. Plaza de Zocodover
8. Museum of La Santa Cruz
9. Alcántara Bridge and Gate
10. Castle of San Servando
11. The Alcázar
12. Mosque of Las Tornerías
13. Town Hall
14. Bishop's Palace
15. Cathedral

Before we enter the old city, a few comments on its layout and town planning. The promontory on which it stands, more or less on seven hills, leading Toledo to be often compared with Rome, is 1.5 kilometres long by 1 kilometre wide. The city's peculiar lie, constantly rising and falling, its labyrinthine narrow streets and its enormous wealth of monuments nevertheless give it much greater dimension. Though encircled by the Tagus, the city was fortified as early as in Roman times. During the Visigoth period, King Wamba reinforced with thick walls the enclosure limited to the north by what is now the Puerta del Sol. Under the Moors, the city, known in those times as *Tulaitula*, grew to the north, expanding outwards to where the Santiago and Antequerela districts now stand in an area protected by walls in which new gates were opened. Opposite the Puerta Vieja de Bisagra, in what is now Avenue de la Caba, was the *maqbara*, or Moslem cemetery. Within the Moorish city proper, the most prominent place was occupied by the alcazaba, the military complex and governor's palace, which stood on the site of what is now the Alcázar. The old Medina also contained the Jewish quarter, forming a highly-differentiated area of the city with its own walls and gates. For their

New Bisagra Gate.

Double patio of the Hospital de Tavera.

part, the Mozarab population co-existed with the Moslems of the city, but were allowed to maintain their churches and practise the old Visigoth liturgy.
With the city's make-up already well-defined, the Christian conquest of 1085 was not followed by any substantial alteration of its lay-out, for one thing because the city was given up, and did not have to be taken by force, so there was no destruction of buildings, and for another due to the admiration felt for Islamic art. From those times onwards, building in Toledo has always been limited by the space available within its walls, and it is not unusual to find the most disparate monuments standing side by side.
We begin this first itinerary at the **New Gate of Bisagra (2)**. The gate is presided over by an enormous imperial coat of arms of the city, with its unmistakable two-headed eagle. Originally Moorish, it was rebuilt in 1550 under the reign of Charles I by Alonso de Covarrubias. The gate has two build-

ings flanking a parade ground. The second body, its front within the walls, has three floors and is crowned by two towers which end in tiled capitals.

Before entering the old city, we can visit the **Tavera Hospital (1),** also known as the Hospital de Afuera, being situated outside the walls. The hospital was founded by Cardinal Tavera, whose magnificent marble tomb, by Alonso Berruguete, occupies a prominent position in the church. The building, completed between 1542 and 1579, is organised around a large courtyard or patio split by an open gallery of two floors, an original arrangement designed by Covarrubias. The left wing of the hospital, which functioned as such up to the Spanish Civil War, now contains the Duque de Lerma Foundation Museum, which houses interesting 16th-centuries furniture and other objects, the excellent hospital library, an apothecary, and a first-rate painting collection, including such works as the famous *Bearded Woman* by Ribera and two paintings by El Greco (a *Holy Family* and the *Portrait of Cardinal Tavera*, as well as *The Saviour*, one of the few sculptures El Greco made).

Now, then, we finally enter the old city, but we do so through

Old Bisagra Gate, or Puerta de Alfonso VI.

Santiago del Arrabal and, in the background, the New Bisagra Gate.

the **Old Gate of Bisagra (3).** Like the New Gate of Bisagra, its name comes from the Arabic *Bab-Shagra*, meaning «Sagra Gate», the gate opening up to the great plains of La Sagra. In order to distinguish it from the New Gate, it is also known as the Alfonso Gate, as it was through this gate that the king Alphonse's army entered the city after the Christian conquest in 1085. Essentially in the Moorish style known as Caliphate, it conserves its original structure, forming an angle and protected by additional turrets. A side entrance leads into a lovely square where a sculpture by Chillida entitled *Lugar de encuentros* («Meeting-place») stands out in peculiar contrast to its surroundings.

Taking Calle Alfonso VI, we come to the Church of **Santiago del Arrabal (4),** one of the finest exponents of Mudéjar art in Toledo. It was built in the 13th century, though its tower dates to the 12th century and may have belonged to a mosque that once stood here. Its ground plan is in the form of a Latin cross,

with nave and two aisles closed by semicircular apses, decorated with a variety of arches in the exterior. Inside, the building features wooden coffering and a fine Plateresque high altar, the work of Francisco de Espinosa.
We now take Calle Real del Arrabal, turning off into the Cuesta del Cristo de la Luz. Crossing the **Puerta de Bab-al-Mardum**, or Valmardón Gate, a 10th-century Moorish work though much altered over time, we find the Mosque of **Cristo de la Luz (5),** the most precious jewel of Islamic art in Toledo, not just because it is preserved practically intact, but also due to its original construction. According to the Cufic inscription on the main front, this tiny building dates to the year 999, though the apse and presbytery were added in the 13th century. Almost square in shape, four columns form the body of the building, with three aisles crossed by three more, creating new spaces, each covered by a vault. The highest of these is the central vault, and all are decorated differently. The columns are crowned by Visigoth capitals, and the arches are Moorish.
Retracing our steps a little, we go down some steps near the Valmardón Gate, from where we can make out, in the wall of the gate, part of the old Roman sewers. Opposite stands the

The Mosque of El Cristo de la Luz.

Puerta del Sol.

Puerta del Sol (6), the most beautiful of all the gates of Toledo. It was built in the 14th century in the Mudéjar style which so characterises the city to facilitate access to the centre from the Arrabal district beyond the walls, offering an alternative to the steep climb carts had to make to enter through the Valmardón Gate. Adjoining the walls, it also served as a military gate. The medallion over the Moorish arch was added in the 16th century and represents the Imposition of the Chasuble on Saint Ildephonse under the moon and the sun («sol»), from which it takes its present name. Further up, among interlacing arches, is a small window and a relief representing the Denial of Saint Peter, from a 4th-century early Christian sarcophagus.
This first itinerary now takes us to the **Paseo del Miradero**, which commands fine views over the countryside and the Antequeruela and Covachuelas districts. This delightful promenade also contains one of the entrances to the **Convent of Santa Fe**, now Provincial Library and Archive. Along with the

dependencies of the Museum of Santa Cruz and the Convent of La Purísima Concepción at the rear, this site is also occupied by the former Galiana Palaces, built by Moslem emirs and whose exquisite ornamentation is said to have been the marvel of all who visited them. All that survives from this period is the 11th-century Chapel of Belén, then a private oratory. The exterior of this small chapel is square in shape, whilst it is chamferred within, and is covered with a Caliphal-style vault.
The Cuesta de las Armas leads into **Plaza de Zocodover (7),** nerve centre of Toledo since Moorish times. Its name derives from the Arabic *Suk-al-Dawab*, meaning market of the beasts. The streets surrounding this square were all full of shops, each devoted to a different product. Even now, the area retains its commercial character, as a walk along Calle Comercio or Calle Hombre de Palo will show. Passing through the **Arco de la Sangre** («Arch of Blood»), where once stood the gate communicating the Medina with the *Al-Hizam* (dwellings of the Moslem governors), we come to Calle Cervantes, where we find the **Museum of La Santa Cruz (8).** The splendid treasures contained here make a visit to this museum almost obligatory.

A view of Plaza de Zocodover with the so-called Arch of Blood.

Main entrance to the former Hospital de la Cruz.

The collections are divided into two sections: Fine Arts (some 20 works by or attributed to El Greco, as well as others by great artists), and Archaeology (with objects dating from prehistory to the Moorish period). Finally, a room devoted to the Decorative Arts contains an exhibition of Toledan popular arts and crafts. The museum is housed in the rehabilitated former Hospital of La Santa Cruz, founded in the late-15th century by Cardinal Pedro González de Mendoza to shelter foundlings and orphans. The work was directed by Enrique and Antón Egas, and Alonso de Covarrubias designed the magnificent main entrance, conceived in the form of a high altarpiece, and the Noble Cloister, including the palatial staircase leading to the upper floor, all in Plateresque style. The building, whose ground plan is in the shape of a Greek cross, has two floors. Inside the main decorative elements are in the coffered ceilings, the crossing and the chapel, which is covered by a ribbed vault.

Before visiting the Alcázar, it is well worth taking a look at the **Alcántara Bridge and Gate (9).** The Alcántara Gate, as its structure reveals, is Moorish in origin. Formerly the main entrance to the *Al-Hizam*, its name derives from the Arabic *Al-Qantara*, meaning bridge, though the bridge already existed in Roman times. Greatly deteriorated, it was rebuilt by the Moors in the late-10th century and later by Alphonse X in 1258 after it was damaged by floods. The west turret dates to this period, though it was altered during the reign of the Catholic Monarchs, whose coat of arms is emblazoned over the arch. For its part, the east turret was replaced in 1721 by a baroque arch. Beyond the bridge, dominating the hillside, is the **Castle of San Servando (10),** Visigoth in origin but completely rebuilt in the 14th century. Its name derives from the Cluniac monastery it housed originally, and which later pertained to the Order of the Knights Templar. In recent years it was rehabilitated to serve as a youth hostel. Returning to the centre, we take

Alcántara bridge and the Castle of San Servando.

Main entrance to the Alcázar, by Alonso de Covarrubias.

The majestic patio of the Alcázar is presided over by a statue of Charles I.

View of the Alcázar from the Alcántara Bridge.

Paseo del Carmen, where there is a lively street market each Tuesday.

The Alcázar (11) stands on the highest hill in the city. Its ever imposing figure has been radically altered over the years since it was first built as the residence of the governors of the city since the days of Roman *Toletum*. The building we now see dates to the reconstruction carried out at the behest of King Charles I in 1535. Nevertheless, it was subsequently completely destroyed by three great fires (during the War of Spanish Succession in 1710, during the War of Independence in 1810 and in 1887, this last fire caused accidentally) and during the famous siege which took place during the Spanish Civil War. Rebuilt exactly as it was when it was Toledo's royal residence, the Alcázar once more houses military dependencies and an interesting and very complete Army Museum.

Taking Calle Horno de los Bizcochos, we go down to Plaza de la Magdalena, a square presided over by the Mudéjar church

Plaza del Ayuntamiento: town hall (left) and Archbishop's Palace (right).

from which it takes its name. In nearby Calle de Las Tornerías, at number 27, stands the **Mosque of Las Tornerías (12).** The mosque, which dates to the 11th century, has a similar structure to that of El Cristo de la Luz, but is more simple. It is thought to have been built as a private oratory, explaining its unusual situation on the upper floor. The site now houses the Castilla-La Mancha Centre for the Promotion of Arts and Crafts.

Passing through Plaza Mayor, presided over by the Teatro Rojas, we take Calle de la Tripería to admire the exceptionally beautiful portal of the Gothic-Mudéjar **Posada de la Hermandad**. The building, which dates to the 14th century, was used as the headquarters of the Holy Brotherhood («Hermandad») until the 19th century, when it was converted into an inn («Posada»). Now rehabilitated as a cultural centre, the building contains the *Sala del Tribunal*.

Skirting the cathedral walls, we come to Plaza del Ayuntamiento,

presided over by the main fronts of the **Town Hall (13),** begun in 1575 according to plans drawn up by Juan de Herrera; the **Bishop's Palace (14),** with its magnificent Flamboyant Gothic style portal; and the **Cathedral (15),** majestic like the rest of the site.
Erected on the same site as that occupied formerly by the Visigoth cathedral and the main mosque, the cathedral began to be built in 1226 at the command of Archbishop Jiménez de Rada during the reign of Ferdinand III the Holy and was substantially completed in 1493. Overall, it is the most monumental and truly autochthonous of all the cathedrals built in Spain during the Gothic period. Its ground plan is in the form of a Latin cross, with nave and four aisles terminating in a double ambulatory, and a

Cathedral: main front.

Cathedral: Puerta de los Leones.

crossing without dome. It is covered by ogee vaults with a large degree of fluing to allow the opening of high windows.
Before entering, however, let us inspect the cathedral exterior. The main front, commenced in 1418, has three doors, all of them greatly decorated. The central is that of the Pardon, whilst on the right is that of the Scribes or of the Final Judgement and on the left is that of the Tower or of the Inferno. The single tower (the second was never built) is crowned by a fine Flamboyant Gothic spire. In the central body of bells is the famous «Campana Gorda» («Fat Bell»), thus-known due to its extraordinary size and weight (17,744 kilos). Taking Calle Arco del Palacio, we pass through the Molleto or Justice Gate into the cloister, which dates to the late-14th century, beautifully decorated with frescoes by Bayeu and Maella between 1776 and 1782. On the north side of the cathedral is the Puerta del Reloj («Clock Door»), adorned with scenes from the life of the Virgin, whilst the south side, in Calle Cardenal Cisneros, contains the Lion Gate («Puerta de los Leones»), a magnificent Flamboyant Gothic work by Enrique Egas, and the Puerta Llana, the most simple of all.

The interior of the cathedral contains a veritable treasure-trove of artistic wonders. The choir is a magnificent Renaissance work, many of the stalls carved by Alonso de Berruguete. The Capilla Mayor, protected by a beautiful grille by Villalpando, is presided over by a colossal Flamboyant Gothic altarpiece. Also outstanding is «El Transparente», a baroque work by Narciso Tomé. This is an altarpiece whose figures seem to float in cloud. The vault above it was broken through to allow daylight to fall on the altar. The Chapterhouse, covered by splendid coffering in the ceiling, contains portraits of all the archbishops of Toledo. In the sacristy is the Cathedral Museum where, under a vault painted by Lucas Jordán, are paintings by El Greco (some 15, including *The Stripping of Christ*) Goya, Van Dyck, Tristán and many more. The Cathedral Treasure, installed in the Chapel of San Juan at the foot of the building, contains such artistic jewels as a large processional monstrance by Enrique Arfe and the magnificently illustrated 13th-century Bible of San Luis.

El Transparente, a baroque painting by Narciso Tomé.

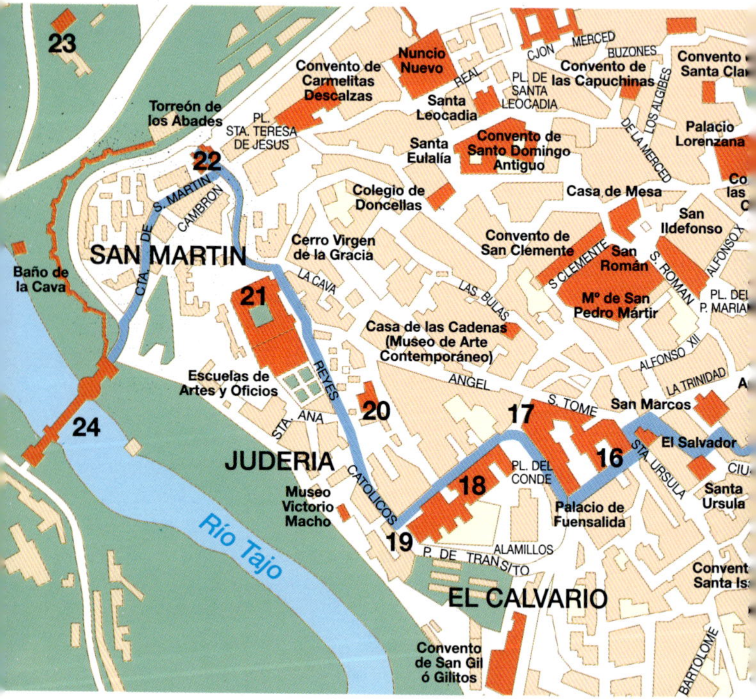

II. THE OLD JEWISH QUARTER AND THE BRIDGE OF SAN MARTÍN

16. El Moro Workshop
17. Church of Santo Tomé
18. El Greco House-Museum
19. El Tránsito Synagogue - Sephardi Museum
20. Synagogue of Santa María la Blanca
21. Monastery of San Juan de los Reyes
22. El Cambrón Gate
23. Hermitage of El Cristo de la Vega
24. Bridge of San Martín

Basically, this second itinerary takes us around the old Jewish quarter of Toledo, home of one of the most influential communities during the medieval period. The quarter was walled, with its own gates and infrastructure (market, baths, schools and synagogues) occupying the larger part of the southeast sector

of the old city. The expulsion of the Jews in 1492 led to the disappearance of the quarter, though the surviving elements nevertheless make this one of the most important in Europe. The remaining heritage of the old Jewish quarter of Toledo include two synagogues and the wicket gate in Calle del Angel, in those days the quarter's main thoroughfare.
From Plaza del Ayuntamiento we pass into Plaza del Consistorio where, in one corner, lies the private Pasadizo del Ayuntamiento, a tiny street whose last section is covered. From here, we enter Calle Ciudad, admiring the 14th-century Gothic-Mudéjar gate which is all that remains of what was once the great Palace of Los Toledo. On the corner stands the **Church of Santa Úrsula**, which belongs to an Augustine convent founded in 1360, to which period the apse dates. The interior is baroque and contains a fine altarpiece by Alonso de Berruguete.
Nearby is the **Church of El Salvador**, a former mosque which was itself built using Visigoth capitals and other elements. An annex building, the Chapel of Santa Catalina, was built in the late-15th century as the burial place of the Alvárez de Toledo family. The most interesting features in the church are the altarpieces, one of them by Pedro de Berruguete.
We now take **Calle Santo Tomé**, where we find one of the best-known symbols of the entire city, the graceful Mudéjar Tower of Santo Tomé, a model of its kind. Before visiting the

Apse of the Church of Santa Ursula.

Calle Santo Tomé with the tower of the same name.

church, however, we take a side turning to the **El Moro Workshop (16)** in Calle Taller del Moro. This has a main room with an alcove on either side, formerly forming part of the adjoining **Palace of Fuensalida**, built in the 14th and 15th centuries. The Workshop is thus known because it was used by craftsmen to produce works both for the cathedral and the city in general. Most of these craftsmen were Moslems or, more exactly, Mudéjars, great experts in the decorative arts. Since 1963, this building has housed a museum of Mudéjar art and crafts which belongs to the Museum of La Santa Cruz. The three rooms are, moreover, finely decorated with magnificent wood coffering and lavish stucco decoration. The main front of the Palace of Fuensalida is in Paseo del Conde, but cannot be visited, as it serves as the Presidential Offices of the Castilla-La Mancha Autonomous Government.

The front of another important monument is also found on Paseo del Conde: the **Church of Santo Tomé (17).** This

church, whose most outstanding element its tower, dates to the 13th century, though it was rebuilt in the 14th. It has a square ground plan and is built of tapered masonry, the two upper floors being of brick. Here are two groups of windows separated by a blind arcade. The observant visitor will also notice other small ornaments, such as the Visigoth cross.
But the most important element in the Church of Santo Tomé is El Greco's painting of *The Burial of the Count of Orgaz*, installed in a room adjoining the entrance from Paseo del Conde. This monumental painting, completed between 1586 and 1588, represents the miracle which occurred in 1312 when Saint Augustine and Saint Stephen appeared at the burial of the count, placing his body in the tomb. The painting was commissioned by the parish, which paid the artist the sum of 1,200 ducats for his work. One of the most interesting

Room in the El Moro Workshop.

The Burial of the Count of Orgaz, considered El Greco's greatest masterpiece, in the Church of Santo Tomé.

aspects of the piece is the gallery of personages attending the funeral. These are portraits of contemporaries of El Greco painted, as in all his works, with great intensity and psychological insight. Amongst them is the artist himself, in the guise of the nobleman looking directly at the spectator, and his son, the page holding a torch and in whose handkerchief is El Greco's signature, in Greek.

Nearby, in Calle Samuel Leví, is the **El Greco House-Museum (18).** In fact, this was never the artist's residence, but a house built in the early-20th century combining a 16th-century building and a Renaissance palace to create a space where El Greco's hither to dispersed work could be brought together. A key role in this initiative was played by the Marquis of Vega-Inclán, who acquired these buildings and furnished them with

authentic 16th-century furniture and other objects. The museum was inaugurated in 1912, and its collection gradually grew in size. The works by El Greco exhibited here correspond, essentially, to his final period of artistic activity, from 1600 to 1614, including his *View and Plan of Toledo* and his *The Twelve Apostles*. An early work, dating to 1585, is the renowned *Tears of Saint Peter*. The museum also contains works from the Toledo School, the Madrid School and the Seville School (17th-century), including works by Luis Tristán, Murillo, Valdés Leal and others.
Domenikos Theotokopuli, known as El Greco, was born in 1541 in Crete, in those times ruled by Venice. He soon moved to Venice and later to Rome, working in both cities with the great Italian masters of the time. Then, like many other Italian artists attracted by the works underway at El Escorial, he arrived in Toledo in 1575-1576, where he received his first commission thanks to the mediation of friends in Rome. From that moment onwards, his name would always be intimately linked with that of Toledo. It was here that he married and where his son was born, here that he developed his personal painting style. Up to his death, in Toledo in 1614,

El Greco House-Museum: The Tears of Saint Peter.

El Tránsito Synagogue, which houses the Sephardi Museum.

he painted over 200 works, most of them scattered around the city and province, but many of them too now in museums all over the world.

Still in Calle Samuel Leví, we find **El Tránsito Synagogue (19),** seat of the **Sephardi Museum**, also known after the name of its founder, Samuel Leví, an important member of the Jewish community of Toledo who became treasurer to King Peter I of Castile. Built in 1356, the synagogue has a rectangular ground plan and is made up of a single nave with the women's gallery in the south wall. The Great Prayer Room is covered by magnificent Mudéjar coffering, whilst the walls are adorned with a fine stucco frieze inscribed with epigraphs in Hebrew and Arabic. The most magnificently decorated is the wall where *hekal* - used to keep the scrolls of the law - is found. After the expulsion of the Jews, the building was consecrated as a Christian church and commended to the Calatrava Order. Since 1964, this has been the incomparable site of the

Sephardi Museum, which offers a complete vision of the history of the Jewish people in Spain, or *Sefarad*, its name in Hebrew, from Roman times to the expulsion in 1492. The museum also contains examples of the cultural production of Sephardi communities scattered all over the world. A second synagogue of the ten once to be found in the Jewish quarter of Toledo and which has survived to our times is the so-called **Synagogue of Santa María la Blanca (20)** in nearby Calle Reyes Católicos. It dates back to the 12th century and has an irregular ground plan with five naves separated by Moorish arches on octagonal pillars with finely-decorated capitals. The synagogue was converted into a Christian church in 1411, and its Plateresque altarpieces were installed at a later date.

At the end of Calle Reyes Católicos stands the **Monastery of San Juan de los Reyes (21),** founded by the Catholic Monarchs to commemorate the victory at the Battle of Toro in 1476 and as their royal pantheon. The conquest of the Moorish Kingdom of Granada in 1492 caused them to change their plans in this respect, however, and the monastery was granted to the Franciscan monks until then installed in what is now the Convent of La Concepción Francisca. Conceived in accord-

Naves of the Synagogue of Santa María la Blanca.

Main entrance of San Juan de los Reyes.

ance with aristocratic, triumphant aesthetic canons, San Juan de los Reyes is a masterpiece of Flamboyant Gothic. Its artifice was Juan Guas, master of the style, also known as *Isabelino* after Queen Isabella. Work began in 1477 and were not completed until the early-16th century. The most outstanding elements are the beautiful cloister, covered by magnificent wood coffering, and the church, with its splendid dome and decoration. The chains outside the church are from Christian captives freed after the conquest of Granada.

We now come to **El Cambrón Gate (22),** completely rebuilt in the 16th century following the same structure as for the New Bisagra Gate. Its name derives from the thorn bush («combronera») which grew on one of the towers. The gate opens into Paseo de Recaredo, peaceful gardens commanding views of the Hermitage of El Cristo de la Vega (23), and the Basilica of Santa Leocadia, a 12th-century hermitage which houses a popular image of the Crucifixion depicting.

San Juan de los Reyes: church.

San Juan de los Reyes: cloister.

Exterior front of El Cambrón Gate.

Crossing El Cambrón Gate once more, we reach the impressive **Bridge of San Martín (24)**, built in the late-13th century to replace an earlier bridge carried away by floods in 1203. Curiously, the bridge retains its two defensive turrets, the outer dating to the 13th century and the inner built in the 16th century. The latter is emblazoned with the imperial coat of arms, flanked by the figure of Emperor Charles V. Nearby is the **Baño de la Cava**, a small turret of Moorish origin which formed part of an old chain ferry.

Presbytery of the Hermitage of Cristo de la Vega, with the popular image of the Crucifixion, the origin of many legends.

Bridge of San Martín and Baño de la Cava.

III. NORTHEAST TOLEDO

25. Plaza de San Vicente
26. Convent of Santo Domingo el Real
27. Palace of the Provincial Government and Mirador de la Granja
28. Church of Santa Leocadia
29. Monastery of Santo Domingo de Silos, «El Antiguo»
30. House of Chains-Museum of Contemporary Art
31. Church of San Román-Museum of the Councils of Toledo and of Visigoth Culture

This third itinerary, like the fourth, takes us to areas of the city which may not be so well-known as others, but are nevertheless full of points of interest. It is precisely strolling the narrow old streets of Toledo which is one of the city's greatest attractions, and to really appreciate its magical atmosphere it is necessary to lose oneself in them. From Plaza del Ayuntamiento, we take Calle Nuncio Viejo and then Alfonso X to **Plaza de San Vicente (25),** where three buildings particularly merit our attention: the Palace of Lorenzana, the Convent of the Agustinas Calzadas and the Church of San Vicente.

The construction of the Palace of Lorenzana, now seat of the Rectorate of Toledo University, was commissioned by Cardinal Lorenzana in the late-18th century and the palace is, therefore, one of the few monumental buildings wholly erected during a period when the city had lost much of its former splendour. Cardinal Lorenzana was one of those activities as a Maecenas did most for the city of Toledo. To him is due the construction of the New University (installed in this palace, though abolished in 1845) and of the new Nuncio, or the restoration of the Archbishop's Palace and many more buildings.

The **Convent of the Agustinas Calzadas**, or of «Las Gaitanas», as it is popularly known, dates to the 15th century, though the interior is much altered. Its most outstanding attraction is the large painting by Ricci which presides over the altar.

Finally, the **Church of San Vicente** is outstanding thanks to its Mudéjar tower and apse. The main front has now been hidden by later constructions. Here, a narrow little street leads us to the peaceful Plaza de Santa Clara, which takes its name from the **Convent of Santa Clara la Real**, whose entrance is at one corner. As this, like all the convents in Toledo, is a convent of cloistered nuns, only the church can be visited during services. Calle Santa Clara leads into Calle Buzones, and here we find one of the most picturesque spots in the entire city: the most

Main doorway of the Palace of Lorenzana.

Work by Ricci in the Convent of the Agustinas Calzadas.

attractive covered passages in Toledo. The austere walls, with scarcely an opening –this is a zone of religious communities– confer even more charm on the place. At the end stands the **Convent of Santo Domingo el Real (26),** recognisable for its entrance porch, one of the largest in the city. The convent was founded in the 14th century, though the present church is baroque. In this tranquil square, two plaques dedicated to Gustavo Adolfo Bécquer render homage to the great Romantic poet and his love of Toledo.

Calle Buzones wends its winding way to Calle de la Merced, from where we see the **Palace of the Provincial Government (27).** This is a 19th-century building which stands on the site of a former monastery of monks of Our Lady of Mercy, destroyed during the French invasion. At the rear of the palace is the **Mirador de la Granja**, the finest viewpoint over the new part of the city.

Nearby is the **Church of Santa Leocadia (28).** This church

conserves its original Mudéjar apses, portal and tower. The interior, much altered, has Renaissance and baroque elements. Adjoining it is the **Monastery of Santo Domingo de Silos, «El Antiguo» (29**), the first to be founded in Toledo after the Christian conquest. Though it features Visigoth remains, the church is Renaissance in style, designed by Juan de Herrera. But what awakens most interest about the monastery is its relation to the painter El Greco, who is buried in the crypt of the church. The Greek genius wished to be laid to rest here because it was in this church that he carried out his first commissioned work in Spain, the high altarpiece. The present altarpiece, however, contains mostly imitations, and only El Greco's original *John the Evangelist* and *The Resurrection of Christ* are conserved, near the epistle. The treasures accumulated over the years by the monastery, including documentation on the life of El Greco, the last will and testament of King Peter I of Castile, gold and silverwork, carvings and paintings, are exhibited in an interesting museum in the choir and other dependencies.
Circling the monastery, we come down to Plaza del Cardenal Suelo, one of whose fronts is occupied by the **Church of**

The Palace of the Diputación (Provincial Government), seen from Avenida de la Caba, and remains of the city walls.

Santa Eulalia, a former Mozarab parish church. Under Moorish rule, the Mozarab population was permitted to continue worshipping in their churches, though no new building was allowed. This tolerant attitude was repeated after the Christian conquest in 1085, in spite of attempts to impose the new Roman liturgy. There were a total of six Mozarab parish churches, founded by the Visigoths, which survived for several centuries: Santa Eulalia, Santa Justa, San Marcos, San Torcuato, San Sebastián and San Lucas. All of them gradually adapted over the years to Roman Christian liturgy, and most of the churches themselves were also rebuilt.

Nearby Calle Colegio de Doncellas owes its name to the centre founded by Cardinal Silíceo in the 16th century. Rebuilt in the 18th century by Ventura Rodríguez, this former girls' school now houses various university dependencies. A walk up the hill known as the **Cerro de la Virgen de la Gracia** allows us to enjoy

Mudéjar tower and apse of the Church of Santa Leocadia.

Main front of the house known as the Casa de las Cadenas, which houses the Contemporary Art Museum.

a fine view of San Juan de los Reyes, just below the viewpoint. We now continue our itinerary through charming little streets until we come to Calle Bulas, where the *Casa de las Cadenas* (**House of Chains, 30)** stands. This building has housed the **Museum of Contemporary Art** since 1975. The 15th-century palace itself constitutes and exceptional example of Mudéjar civil architecture. It is a three-storey building arranged around a central courtyard or patio, and is finely decorated with floral motifs and inscriptions.

Taking Calle San Clemente, and accompanied by noble old walls, we reach Plaza San Román. The walls correspond to the former **Convent of San Clemente** (with fine Plateresque portal by Alonso de Covarrubias), that of **San Pedro Mártir**

Museum of the Councils of Toledo and of Visigoth Culture, installed in the Church of San Román.

(now rehabilitated as administrative offices) and the **Church of San Román**, which houses the **Museum of the Councils of Toledo and of Visigoth Culture (31).** The museum, as its name indicates, contains collections of different objects from the period, such as codexes, gold and silverwork and jewellery. Moreover, the Church of San Román is itself Visigoth in origin, conserving various original capitals as well as the crypt. The church was used as a mosque during the period of Moorish domination, but the building is basically Mudéjar, dating to the early-13th century. Perhaps its finest element is the graceful tower of the church, which was the highest in the city until that of the cathedral was completed. The church also features fine Romanesque mural paintings, amongst very few examples of this type of art to be found in the entire region of Castile.
Plaza San Román is one of the most beautiful locations in Toledo. A statue of Garcilaso de la Vega (1503-1536), an

outstanding figure in Spanish literature, born in Toledo, was recently added to the monuments above described. From the square, we can also visit the so-called **Casa de Mesa**, an old Mudéjar palace which has been greatly altered over the years but which conserves magnificent stucco decoration in the interior. The main doorway, Renaissance in style, stands exactly opposite the Church of San Román.
This third itinerary ends in Plaza del Padre Mariana, at the end of Calle San Román. This square is presided over by the **Church of San Ildefonso**, or of San Juan Bautista, as it is also known, having been thus denominated up to the year 1900. It was then consecrated to Saint Ildephonse because it was believed that the church occupied the site of the house where the Toledan archbishop was born. Built between the 17th and 18th centuries, the church is typical of Jesuit construction, both in its proportions and its decoration.

Mudéjar art in the Casa de Mesa.

IV. SOUTHERN TOLEDO

32. Convent of Santa Isabel
33. «Palace of Rey Don Pedro»
34. Church of San Andrés
35. Church of San Sebastián
36. Casa del Diamantista
37. Church of San Lucas
38. Convent of San Juan de la Penitencia
39. Church of Santos Justo y Pastor

This final itinerary also begins in Plaza Ayuntamiento, taking Calle Santa Isabel, at the end of which is a Mudéjar building, the **Convent of Santa Isabel (32),** founded in 1477 by Doña María Suárez de Toledo, who donated various family palaces for its construction. To these properties was added the Parish Church of San Antolín during the reign of the Catholic Monarchs, from which a late-12th-century Mudéjar apse is conserved. The interior of the church –the only space open to the public– is Gothic in style, with a fine Renaissance-style high altarpiece.

Adjoining the convent is a square which takes its name from the **Palace of Rey Don Pedro (33),** thus known although it never actually belonged to King Peter. Dating to the 14th century, the building has a fine portal in the style of Toledan palaces, emblazoned with the coats of arms of the founders. Nearby, adjoining the enormous building housing the Seminary, is the **Church of San Andrés (34),** one of the most interesting in the city, as it unites elements from all periods. It was a Visigoth church (various pilasters and capitals are conserved), then a mosque (a funeral stone from the Moorish period is also kept here) before the head of the church was rebuilt in Late-Gothic style in around 1500. In it are fine Plateresque altarpieces by Juan de Borgoña, whilst the main doorway also merits attention. In Almohade style, it is unique of its type in Toledo.

Descending the steep streets of Calle Sola and Calle Santa Catalina, we come to the **Church of San Sebastián (35),**

Convent of Santa Isabel.

Church of San Andrés.

Almohade portal of the Church of San Andrés.

formerly a Mozarab parish church. Nevertheless, various elements, such as the absence of apses reveal that it was formerly a mosque. It has a nave and two aisles, separated by Moorish arches supported by columns with Roman and Visigoth capitals. The tower is Mudéjar, the result of large-scale alterations in the 15th century.

Taking Carrera de San Sebastián, we pause at the corner with Bajada del Barco. The path downwards leads to the house known as the **Casa del Diamantista (36).** This typical rambling old house stands in a lovely spot on the banks of the Tagus near a jetty where a ferry takes us to the other side of the river. Here, a path leads to the **Hermitage of La Virgen del Valle**, but which is only used for the popular *romería*, religious procession, on May 1 each year. This was, however, for centuries, the traditional route to the hermitage, though it can now be reached from the ring road, or Carretera de Circunvalación. The main attraction of taking this route lies in the magnificent view obtained of the old city from the view-

Church of San Sebastián.

Jetty beside the house known as the Casa del Diamantista.

point («mirador»), and from the **Parador Nacional** (state-run hotel) situated higher up the mountain.
Continuing along Carrera de San Sebastián, we come to the **Church of San Lucas (37),** considered the oldest of the Mozarab parish churches of Toledo, though it is now made up of a series of buildings from different periods. The tower has an unmistakably Mudéjar silhouette, whilst in the interior, large-scale restoration work revealed the most important feature of the church: various Gothic mural paintings.
We now return to the centre, stopping at the former **Convent of San Juan de la Penitencia (38)** in the street of the same name. This was founded by Cardinal Cisneros in 1514 as the Poor Girls' School. It was damaged by fire in 1936 and was restored recently. It now houses university dependencies. Practically adjoining the convent is the **Church of Santos Justo y Pastor (39)**, another interesting exponent of Toledan Mudéjar art.

Bajada de San Justo and the tower of the same name.

Church of San Lucas.

Toledan sweetmeats.

GASTRONOMY

For starters, *pisto manchego, tortilla a la magra, migas, gazpacho* or *sopa castellana* (vegetable hash, omelette, fried breadcrumbs, soup). Main courses: partridge, quail, wild boar, trout or *carcamusas* (venison). These are the most characteristic dishes of the cuisine of Toledo. This is an eminently rural cuisine, which takes something from all the cultures which have been present in these lands, rich in agriculture as well as in big and small game. And as for desserts, there is the famous marzipan, available here not only at Christmas, or *toledanas* (filled with vermicelli), not to mention the local cheeses, particular Manchegos, whether made from pure sheep's milk or, like the *añejos,* cured in oil. Regarding wine, there are two DOCs in the province, La Mancha and Méntrida, rarely stronger than 15° proof.

ARTS AND CRAFTS

The most celebrated crafts of Toledo are swordmaking and damascening, both of which activities have long-standing traditions here. The swordmaking industry or, better, the Toledo steel industry, as it also includes the magnificent medieval armour we can admire in many shops, goes back to the times of the Visigoths, and only began to decline with the advent of firearms. For its part, damascening, the art of decorating iron or steel with inlaid work of precious metals, was introduced by the Moors, and was used particularly to adorn swords and armour. Also rightly-famed is the pottery of Talavera de la Reina and El Puente del Arzobispo. This is hand-decorated glazed, polychrome ceramic. Finally, lovely embroidery is produced in Lagartera, hand-made by the patient women of that city since the 16th century.

Damascening is one of the most traditional crafts in Toledo.

Festivity of Corpus Christi.

POPULAR FESTIVITIES AND TRADITIONS

The people of Toledo being great lovers of liturgy and ritual, the local festivities are all highly ceremonious. The most important and deeply-rooted of these is the feast of **Corpus Christi**, which takes place between the end of May and the beginning of June each year. This festivity, famed all over the world, has been declared of Tourist Interest. The ritual has been conserved practically unchanged over the centuries. During the week previous to the procession led by the monumental monstrance with the Holy Sacrament, the streets along the route are protected by awnings, the balconies of the houses are all decorated with flags, flowers and tapestries, and historic old tapestries are also hung from the outer walls of the cathedral. The night before the procession, the *carrera* is inaugurated by the local dignitaries, accompanied by crowds of locals and visitors alike. This committee is preceded by the «Pertiguero», who uses a pole as high as the monstrance to ensure that the awnings are all at the correct height. Finally, the solemn procession takes place. The whole ceremony is a spectacular affair, from the cross which is carried at the head of the religious parade, made in the 16th century of gold and silver, donated by King Alphonse VI, to the costumes worn by the participants, traditional robes reaching down to the ground, covered with herbs, thyme and rosemary. The procession is preceded by *gigantes y cabezudos*, «giants» and «big heads», who open up a path through the crowd with their dancing. Whilst Corpus Christi is a fiesta of light and colour, **Holy Week** in Toledo, though not enjoying the same renown, is also a moving spectacle due to its austere beauty. Of the local *romerías*, religious processions in honour of a particular saint, moreover, we can mention particularly that in honour of the Virgen del Valle on May 1. On this day, the hermitage bell rings out all day for, according to tradition, «If you don't ring the bell, you'll never marry». The patron saint of Toledo is the Virgin of the Sagrary, festivities in whose honour are held each August 15 with a large programme of events and a fair.

In the rest of the province, particularly interesting is **Corpus Christi in Camuñas**. Here, a peculiar «dance-fight» is performed, medieval in origin and symbolising the «triumph of Grace over Evil». The event is organised by two brotherhoods («sins» and «dancers»), dressed in traditional costume, some wearing horned masks and others masks with long, thin noses.

Corpus Christi in Camuñas.

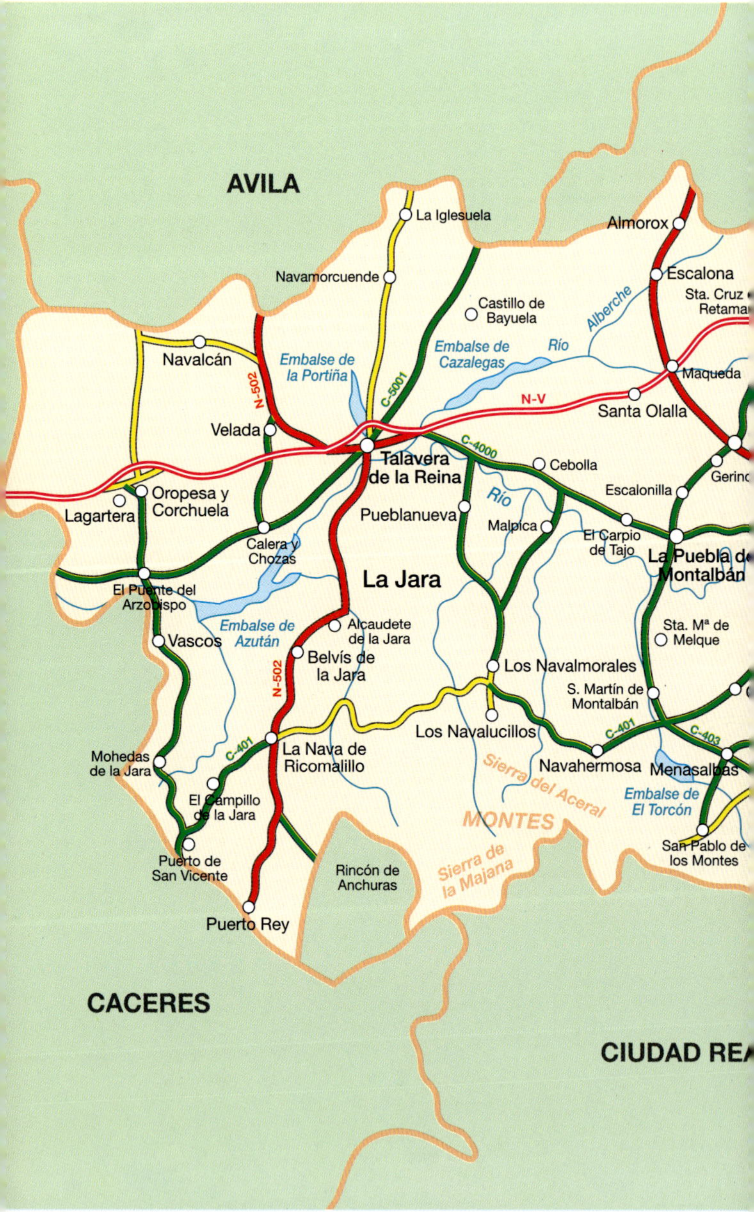
AVILA
La Iglesuela
Almorox
Navamorcuende
Escalona
Castillo de Bayuela
Sta. Cruz Retamar
Alberche
Navalcán
Embalse de la Portiña
Embalse de Cazalegas
Río
Maqueda
N-502
C-5001
N-V
Santa Olalla
Velada
C-4000
Talavera de la Reina
Cebolla
Oropesa y Corchuela
Lagartera
Río
Escalonilla
Pueblanueva
Malpica
El Carpio de Tajo
Calera y Chozas
La Puebla de Montalbán
La Jara
El Puente del Arzobispo
Embalse de Azután
Alcaudete de la Jara
Sta. Mª de Melque
Vascos
Belvís de la Jara
N-502
Los Navalmorales
S. Martín de Montalbán
Los Navalucillos
C-401
C-403
C-401
La Nava de Ricomalillo
Mohedas de la Jara
Navahermosa
Menasalbas
Sierra del Aceral
El Campillo de la Jara
Embalse de El Torcón
MONTES
Puerto de San Vicente
Rincón de Anchuras
Sierra de la Majana
San Pablo de los Montes
Puerto Rey
CACERES
CIUDAD REA

MADRID
almojado
Carranque
Illescas
Seseña
Esquivias
Borox
Recas
Cobeja
Pantoja
Yuncler
Villaluenga
de la Sagra
Olías del Rey
Añover
de Tajo
Mocejón
N-401
LEDO
Villasequilla
Río Algodor
Nambroca
Almonacid
Ajofrín
C-400
Mora
Sonseca
Orgaz
Los Yébenes
TOLEDO
C-400
N-401
Urda
Consuegra
Madridejos
Camuñas
Villafranca de
los Caballeros
Sierra Morrones
Mesa
de
Ocaña
Yepes
Huerto de
Valdecarrábanos
Noblejas
Villarrubia de
Santiago
Ocaña
Santa Cruz
de la Zarzal
Dosbarrios
Villatobas
N-301
C-3000
CUENCA
La Guardia
Corral de
Almaguer
C-402
Tembleque
Lillo
Riansares
N-IV
C-402
La Villa de
Don Fadrique
Villacañas
Río
La Puebla de
Almoradiel
Quero
Miguel Esteban
El Tobos

The Castle of Peñas Negras in Mora.

I. CASTLE ROUTE

The imposing castles of Toledo province are robust symbols of other times, of battle and conquest. Some are now in ruins, whilst others are well conserved, some are Moorish in origin, whilst others were built more recently. This route will take us principally to the castles of the south, finally leading us to Escalona in the north. This is a long journey which also includes such interesting localities as Melque, where we will visit the oldest church in the province.
Heading towards La Mancha along the C-400, the first point of interest we come to is **Almonacid**. The castle, which stands on the peak of a hill, already existed in Moorish times. It then passed into the hands of the Church of Toledo and later became privately owned, when it fell into neglect. Legend has it that this was the regular residence of the Cid, as well as serving as the prison of Prince Alphonse during the reign of John I of Castile.

Our next stop is in **Mora**, in the heart of an olive oil producing region. The Late-Gothic parish church was the scene of a tragic page in the history of the War of the Communities in 1520 when more than one thousand local people were burned alive in it. Mora Castle, known as the Castle of Peñas Negras, stands outside the town on the Tembleque road. Though much deteriorated, the climb up is rewarded by magnificent panoramic views over Mora and the surrounding countryside.
We now take the C-402 local road to **Orgaz**, ten kilometres from Mora. Lying in the foothills of the Montes de Toledo, Orgaz is said to be the birthplace of Doña Jimena, wife of the Cid, who was, according to legend, its first mayor. Orgaz has a beautiful Churrigueresque parish church containing a copy of El Greco's *The Stripping of Christ*. The castle, built in the late-14th century, has been well restored. The entrance is emblazoned with the coat of arms of the Count of Orgaz, who ordered the castle's construction.
We now return to Toledo to take the C-401 local road, which takes us to **Guadamur**. This town, Moorish in origin, has an excellent fortress dating to the late-14th century, built by the first Count of Fuensalida and restored in the 1940s by the

Guadamur: Castle and Hermitage of La Virgen de la Natividad.

Santa María de Melque.

present owners who open the castle to visitors on public holidays. Close to the fortress is the Hermitage of the Virgen de la Natividad, which takes its name from the hill on which both monuments stand and is a simple but charming Mudéjar construction.

There are another two castles in **Polán**, just three kilometres from Guadamur, and **Cuerva**, a little further, though they retain little of their former glory. One which does conserve all its majesty, however, is **Montalbán Castle**, the most impressive in the entire province. To reach it, turn left outside San Martín de Montalbán, though the road is closed six days a week from February 1 to May 16 as protected eagles build their nests in this area, and is open on Saturdays only. The castle is a monumental work standing on the banks of the Torcón, protected on the other side by a great precipice and built, it is thought, by the Knights Templar. The castle's defences also include moat and barbican.

Nearby, on the other side of the road, is the **Church of Santa María del Melque**, Visigoth in origin and the oldest and best-conserved in the province, as well as one of the finest exponents of Visigoth architecture in Spain. The church formed part of a monastery dating to the late-9th century. Small in size, its ground plan is in the shape of a Greek cross and is built in ashlar masonry and covered by vaults supported by Moorish arches.
Our route now continues along the same road to **La Puebla de Montalbán**, an important market town well-known as the birthplace of Fernando de Rojas, author of *La Celestina*. The 16th-century naturalist Francisco Hernández, whose work *Historia Plantarum Novae Hispaniae* describes his experience in the West Indies, was also born here. The town has a beautiful Plaza Mayor, prototype of the Castilian square. In the square stands a fine ducal palace with Plateresque doorway and the Church of Nuestra Señora de la Paz, Gothic with Renaissance elements.
From La Puebla de Montalbán, the 4000 local road takes us to **Malpica de Tajo**, some 20 kilometres away. Standing in beautiful surroundings, the Mudéjar castle is well-conserved. With a square ground plan, it has four towers. In 15th century,

Puebla de Montalbán: Plaza Mayor.

Plateresque doorway to the Collegiate Church of the Santísimo Sacramento in Torrijos.

the castle passed into the possession of captain-general Pedro de Ribera.
The next stop is **Torrijos**, some 15 kilometres to the north of La Puebla de Montalbán. At this important rural district capital we can visit the interesting Collegiate Church of El Santísimo Sacramento, whose building was ordered in 1510 by the lord of Maqueda and his wife, Teresa Enríquez, popularly known as «the madwoman of El Sacramento». The most interesting features of the building are the superb Plateresque west door and the graceful tower. Inside, the church has fine choirstalls and an altarpiece, both dating to the 16th century. Also worth seeing in Torrijos is the Plaza Mayor, flanked by noble palaces,

the Hospital de la Caridad, housed in a Renaissance building, and, in the outskirts, the Convent of Franciscan Conceptionists. Here are recumbent statutes of the lord and lady of Maqueda, who also founded the convent.
Just five kilometres from Torrijos is **Barcience**, a tiny village with a castle on the hilltop. This fortress dates back to the 14th century and once belonged to the Portuguese Silva family, which supported King John I in his moves to unit Spain and Portugal. The most outstanding feature of the castle is the great escutcheon of the Silvas –a lion rampant– in the Keep, in turn one of the most curious examples of Spanish heraldry.
Taking N-403, we now come to the town of **Maqueda**, twelve kilometres from Torrijos. The remains of the old walls bear witness to the fact that this was a key strategic point during Moorish times. The town then fell into Christian hands, and King Alphonse VI resided in the castle when he was preparing for the conquest of Toledo. Later proprietors included Don Alvaro de Luna, Cardinal Mendoza and Isabella the Catholic, until it was finally acquired by the dukes of Maqueda. The castle was built in the 15th century on the site of the old Moorish alcazaba. It has a regular ground plan and impressive cylindrical towers. The parish church is Mudéjar, whilst other important local monuments are the Hermitage of San Silvestre, built in the 17th century and, nearby, a 15th-century column

Barcience Castle.

Escalona Castle.

known as «*Rollo de la Justicia*». Visitors on April 27 should not miss the magnificent enactment of the battles between Moors and Christians celebrated in honour of the patron saint of Maqueda, the Virgin of the Die.

Some thirteen kilometres to the north is **Escalona**, an interesting medieval town on the banks of the Alberche. Escalona still conserves part of its city walls, built during Moorish times, the Church of San Miguel rising from one of the old gates. The 16th-century Convent of La Encarnación has Plateresque portal and cloister, whilst the arcaded Plaza Mayor is famed as the scene of one of the chapters of the novel *Lazarillo of Tormes*, when the young Lázaro abandons the blind miser to his fate, striking him a sound blow. Nevertheless, the main attraction of Escalona is its castle. Built by Alvaro de Luna in the 15th century, this Mudéjar castle was one of the most impressive of its time. The fortress having lost much of its splendour during the War of Independence, restoration work continues on it.

Maqueda: the parish church and the Moorish gate in the old city walls.

Maqueda Castle.

Seseña: Puñoenrostro Castle.

II. LA SAGRA AND TOLEDAN LA MANCHA

To the north of Toledo province stretches La Sagra *comarca* (rural district) for the most part a region of plains and steppe. Its capital, **Illescas**, some 30 kilometres from Toledo along the Madrid dual carriageway, is our main point of interest in La Sagra. Here, we can admire one of the most beautiful Mudéjar towers in the province, known as the Giralda of La Sagra and pertaining to the Church of Santa María, built in the 13th and 14th centuries. Another of the attractions of Illescas is the church of the Hospital de la Caridad, which contains five paintings by El Greco. Of the old Moorish walls which formerly encircled the town there remains the Ugena Gate, built in the 11th century. We can find even older remains in Santa María de Abajo in nearby **Carranque**: the ruins of a 4th-century Roman villa.
Some six kilometres to the east stands **Seseña** and Puñoenrostro Castle, a 14th-century fortress with a large keep. The

Illescas: Ugena Gate.

Carranque: Roman ruins in Santa María de Abajo.

Ocaña: Plaza Mayor.

Seseña road also passes through **Esquivias**, birthplace of Catalina Salazar Palacios, wife of Miguel de Cervantes. Here they married and lived for a time in a house which is still conserved. This is a typical 16th-century rambling old house with two storeys and a lovely patio.
From Seseña, we take the dual carriageway through Aranjuez in Madrid province to **Ocaña**, once more in Toledo province. The origins of this town, capital of La Mesa de Ocaña *comarca*, go back to ancient Carpetania, when it was known as *Ulcania*. The Roman road from Merida to Saragossa is also known to have passed through Ocaña. During the period of Moorish rule, the town was given by Aben-Abed, Emir of Seville, to King Alphonse VI as the dowry of his daughter Zaida on their marriage. After the Christian conquest of Toledo in 1085, it was granted to the Order of Santiago, becoming the principal centre of commerce in the *comarca*. Ocaña has an eminently medieval air, and conserves excellent convents and palaces. Particularly attractive are the

Plaza Mayor, without doubt one of the most beautiful in Spain, built by King Charles III in 1777, and the so-called Fuente Grande or Fuente Nueva, a monumental fountain built in Herreran style in the 16th century. The construction has two sections, the fountain proper and the wash house, a large basin into which water flows from ten spouts. This space is sheltered by a large porticoed gallery with Tuscan columns.

Another important town in La Sarga is **Yepes**, which lies eleven kilometres from Ocaña. Yepes is listed as a place of Historic Interest due to the beauty of the buildings and monuments. Particularly impressive is the Church of San Benito, one of the finest in the entire province. It was built in the 16th century according to the plans drawn up by Alonso de Covarrubias. San Benito is a church of large proportions, with nave and two aisles and fourteen chapels. Nevertheless, its most outstanding element is the High Altarpiece, the work of

Yepes: Church of San Benito.

Tembleque: a view of Plaza Mayor.

Luis Tristán, a follower of El Greco. A tower and three gates are preserved of the old city walls which formerly encircled Yepes. We now resume our journey into the Toledan part of La Mancha, though many geographers in fact place La Mesa de Ocaña district in La Mancha Alta. Nevertheless, the typical features of the landscape associated with La Mancha –broad plains dotted with windmills, white villages, farmhouses, olives and vines– are more a constant of the southeast of the province. From Ocaña, still on the dual carriageway, **La Guardia**, famed for its houses carved into the rock, is well worth a visit. The Chapel of La Concepción in the Church of La Asunción is magnificently decorated with frescoes by Angelo Nardi. Some ten kilometres further along the road is **Tembleque**, a town built around a magnificent, highly original Plaza Mayor. It

dates to the 17th century, when it was built on the site of an earlier square, and has beautiful decoration in the form of a frieze in the galleries. Other monuments of interest are the Renaissance parish church and the baroque constructions of the «Casa de las Torres» («House of Towers») and the Hermitage of El Cristo del Valle.
From Tembleque we make for **Villacañas**, where we can visit various *silos*, dwellings excavated into the rock, adapting to the terrain, like those we saw previously in La Guardia. Finally, in **Quintanar de la Orden** we take the turn-off to **El Toboso**, a town immortalised in *Don Quixote* as the home of the protagonist's beloved Dulcinea. The House of Dulcinea, open to the public, a typical Castilian farmhouse, adds credence to the theory that Cervantes' heroine really existed. The Cervantes Centre in the town also possesses a complete collection of the work of the great writer, with old editions and more modern versions, translated into over 30 languages.

El Toboso: Church of San Antonio Abad and the monument to Don Quixote and Dulcinea.

Consuegra: windmills and the castle.

Heading towards Toledo once more, we pass through **Camuñas**, famed for its festivities at Corpus Christi, and **Consuegra**, one of the most typical villages of the Toledan part of La Mancha. Consuegra lies at the foot of the hill known as the *Cerro Calderico*, its crest marked by a row of windmills and at the top of which stands a castle built in the 12th century by the Order of Saint John. The windmills of Consuegra, like most of those in La Mancha, no longer serve the purpose for which they were built, and few still conserve their original machinery. One which does is the mill known as *Sancho*, which starts up on the occasion of the *Fiesta de la Rosa del Azafrán* («Festivity of the Saffron Rose»), in the last week of October. The events forming part of this festival, declared as being of Tourist Interest, includes a National Saffron-Peeling Competition. The other windmills here house the local tourist information office, craft exhibitions and an extensive collection of Don Quixote in various languages, including a Braille edition, in the mill known as «El Caballero del Verde Gabán». In the centre of Consuegra are various interesting buildings: the Church of El Santísimo Cristo, which dates to the late-18th century; the Town Hall, built in Renaissance style; the buildings known as the *Corredores*, which house the Municipal Museum; and the 16th-century Church of San Juan. In the outskirts are Roman remains - Consuegra even had a Roman circus. These remains are found five kilometres along the Urda road, and consist of a dam which was 800 metres in length and five metres in height.

Finally, another 14 kilometres along the road, we come to **Los Yébenes**, a site popular with hunters as it lies in the foothills of the Montes de Toledo. This lovely town has two churches, that of Santa María, with Mudéjar decoration, and that of San Juan, with a graceful tower. In nearby Fuentes Secas are the remains of a Roman aqueduct, whilst in the Guadalerzas Valley is a castle dating back to the 12th century.

Consuegra: Church of El Santísimo Cristo.

Talavera de la Reina.

III. TALAVERA DE LA REINA AND OROPESA

At the meeting of the River Tagus with the Alberche, a fertile, well-communicated zone, is **Talavera de la Reina**, the most highly-populated city and the industrial and commercial capital of the province. Its origins go back to the remote times of Carpetania, when it was known as *Aebura*, whilst it was the *Caesarobriga* of Roman times, *Ebora* under the Visigoths and, finally, *Talabayra* during the period of Moorish domination, from which its present name derives. The addition of «de la Reina» («of the Queen») is due to the fact that on marrying María of Portugal in 1328, Alphonse XI gave her, amongst other wedding gifts, the city of Talavera. Later, in 1369, Henry II granted sway over it to the arbishopric of Toledo in return for the town of Alcaraz, and Talavera became the centre of an extensive feudal estate. It was during the 16th century that the local ceramists began to earn fame for their work, and Talavera is now known as the «City

of Ceramics» *par excellence*. The Ruiz de Luna Museum contains a magnificent collection of ceramic from Talavera, illustrating its evolution over the centuries. Particularly interesting are the works gathered together over the years by the renowned ceramist Ruiz de la Luna and which he donated to the city.
Regarding the artistic and architectural heritage of Talavera, we can begin by admiring the remains of the old city walls, which date back to three different historic periods, the first section built in the 10th century. The Plaza del Pan was remodelled in 1579 and later embellished by the installation of ceramic works by Ruiz de Luna, and other interesting monuments include the Church of Santiago, built in the 14th century on the site of a former synagogue; the building formerly occupied by the Hieronymite Convent of Santa Catalina (now San Prudencio), with magnificent Renaissance church; the baroque convents of San Bernardo and San Agustín el Viejo (which now houses the Ruiz de Luna Museum) and the medieval Old Bridge («Puente

Talavera de la Reina: Collegiate Church of Santa María la Mayor.

Talavera de la Reina: Plaza del Pan and the town hall.

Viejo»). The Collegiate Church of Santa María la Mayor and the Basilica of La Virgen del Prado deserve mention apart. The former, which stands in Plaza del Pan, is Gothic-Mudéjar in style. With rectangular ground plan, it has a nave and two aisles without crossing. The main front features a magnificent rose window. The cloister was built in the late-15th century, whilst the two upper sections of the tower were added at the beginning of the 18th. For its part, the Basilica of La Virgen del Prado, dedicated to the patron saint of the city, stands at the entrance to the city. Originally a hermitage, the building, which dates to 1570, was extended in the mid-17th century by the addition of the crossing and dome, a fine baroque work by Fray Lorenzo de San Nicolás. Nevertheless, the most interesting aspect of the church is the covering of the walls by artistic panels of *azulejos*, decorated tiles, from the 16th to the 20th century, making the building a veritable museum of local ceramics.
An interesting excursion from Talavera de la Reina is to the

quite villages and beautiful mountain landscapes of the Sierra de San Vicente to the north. In the midst of this scenery, in striking contrast to La Mancha, is **Navamorcuende**, which has a magnificent church, built using the finest masonry throughout by Pedro de Tolosa in the 16th century.
Retracing our route back to Talavera de la Reina, we now take the Extremadura road some 40 kilometres to **Oropesa**, whose origins also go back to pre-Roman times. This noble town contains various interesting civil and religious monuments, including the walled enclosure, with one-and-a-half kilometres of wall, the 15th-century town hall, the Clock Tower, built in early 20th century, the Roman bridge over the Guadyerbas, the beautiful Jesuit Church of San Bernardo, with its fine Plateresque doorway, the Flamboyant Gothic Parish Church of La Asunción and various convents. But Oropesa's most representative monument is, without doubt, its castle. This is a monumental site going back to the 12th century, when the original fortress was built. A new castle

Oropesa: Clocktower.

Oropesa Castle, now a Parador Nacional.

was completed in the 15th century, so that there are two parade grounds separated by a stretch of wall. Adjoining the castle is the palace which was the residence of the Alvárez de Toledo family up to the 18th century, since 1931 a *Parador Nacional* (one of a chain of state-run hotels), one of the finest in Spain.
Oropesa is also a centre for craftwork, particularly embroidery Nevertheless, its fame does not match that of nearby **Lagartera**, where the local women can often be seen sewing in the sun, especially in winter.
Some 13 kilometres from Oropesa is **El Puente del Arzobispo**, whose name alludes to Archbishop Don Pedro Tenorio, who ordered a bridge over the Tagus to be built in the 14th century, and it was around this that the town grew up. El Puente del Arzobispo contains many interesting and well conserved examples of popular architecture, but it is most famed for its ceramic industry which, different from Talavera, is characterised by the use of green tones over a white background and the depiction of hunting scenes.

Lagartera: Monument to La Lagarterana.

El Puente del Arzobispo: Plaza de España and the Church of Santa Catalina.

CONTENTS

EDITORIAL ESCUDO DE ORO, S.A.
I.S.B.N. 84-378-1950-4
Printed by FISA - Escudo de Oro, S.A.
Palaudarias, 26 - 08004 Barcelona
Dep. Legal B. 32207-2005